James Whitney

The tale of the children of Lamech

A poem

James Whitney

The tale of the children of Lamech
A poem

ISBN/EAN: 9783337137526

Printed in Europe, USA, Canada, Australia, Japan

Cover: Foto ©Andreas Hilbeck / pixelio.de

More available books at **www.hansebooks.com**

BY

JAMES A. WHITNEY, LL.D.

NEW YORK:

N. TIBBALS & SONS,

124 Nassau Street.

1885.

TO THE MEMORY OF MY FATHER,

AMAZIAH WHITNEY,

WHO DIED THIRTY YEARS AGO,

A MAN OF KINDLY HEART AND GENTLE WAYS,

WHO, FROM YOUTH TO AGE,

FEARED GOD AND KEPT HIS COMMANDMENTS,

THIS VOLUME

' IS REVERENTLY INSCRIBED.

THE TALE OF THE

CHILDREN OF LAMECH.

Not yet the memory of Eden lost
Had faded from the tribes whose scatter'd paths
Threaded the plain of Shinar.   In their veins
Still ran the juices of the bitter fruit
Borne by the tree of life : so centuries
Must come to men ere yet their wasting strength
Bade them remember that the Lord had said
That dust from Earth must unto Earth return.
And generations seven from the loins
Of Adam sprang and peopled the new land

Beyond the Gihon.   And still Adam walked,

Though broken with deep delving of the ground

And wearied with old sorrows unforgot,

Among the sons of men.   And in his age

Watched with the sheep of Enoch and his sons,

Yet ever looked he eastward to the walls

Of the dark city in the land of Nod

That evil Cain had builded.

In that day

All they were shepherds who from Seth had sprung,

Seth, who had come because of Abel slain,

For theirs the heritage of Abel's flocks

And Abel's peaceful ways, and Abel's lore

Of what the skies foretold, and whence the wind

Came driving fleecy clouds that to the herbs

Gave nourishing of rain.   And to and fro

And round about the pastures grazed the flocks,

Yet ever turning, so that far away

Against the sky the city rose to view:

And all around its walls the fields were green
With thrift of tillage. . When the plains were brown
In the parched summer the far slopes gave forth
A growing glimmer of soft gold, and soon
The yellow harvests shone.

          And so the sons
Of Seth were shepherds on the pasture plain.
And those of Cain were toilers in the hills.

Ever upon the plain when fell the night
And flocks were gather'd close, the wand'rers saw
The calm clear stars shine thro' the azure sky :
And saw that some were steadfast in their place,
Unchanging and unchanged ; and chief of these
The one that glowed unfailing o'er the hills
From which the rivers flowed. And others marked
That slowly swept the heavens night by night,
Changing from what they were, yet sought again
The place from whence they came : and most of all

Of these the star that broader shone anear
The even and the dawn.

              The solitude
Was filled with wondrous silence, and they dreamed
To mark the pathways of the skies and know
The marvel of the stars.   And year by year
Their wisdom grew : and so foretold the days,
The coming of the seasons, of the rain
To quench the desert drouth, the aridness
When heaven's windows should be shut and so
The wrath of the high sun should smite the earth :
And forecast all the comings of the winds.
Upon broad stones they marked the thrones of all
The stars that steadfast were; and marked the
      course
Of those that went upon appointed ways ;
So that Seth's sons and daughters knew the paths
Trod by the hosts of heaven.

In the hills
The toilers delved the earth and searched the mold,
Seeking the secret of each seed that swelled
And sprang to leaf and stem.   Observantly
They saw the slow unwearied spiders spin,
The fox his dwelling dig, the bird its nest
Build deftly in the branches.   Of each herb
They marked the hidden virtue, and each tree
To them gave knowledge.   And they wrought their
        tasks,
Each diligent to learn the secret craft
Whereby or bird or beast or insect kept
Its place within the world, for like to these
They dwelt within the land.   From out the earth
To them came lore of safety, and its fruits
Were plenteous to them.   And so the sons
Of Cain had knowledge of the woods and fields.
And ever from the hills the toilers marked
The idling shepherds on the lands below.
And ever by their sheep the shepherds told

Loud scornful tales of those upon the hills.
Yet back and forth the traders came and went,
For these the fruitage of the hills required,
While those had need of yield from out the flocks. .
And often, envious, to the golden land
Where the blithe harvests waved, the lowland swains
Gazed eastward from the plain.   And from the slopes
Of the high fields the tillers paused to see
The lowland maidens wait the sheep beside,
That grazed upon the wastes.

              And in that day,
Saving of Abel slain, no death had come
Unto the seed of Adam.

              Cain had gone,
His city builded, from among his sons,
Nor knew they whence or whither : oftentimes
Alike on plain and hillside came the tale
Of who had seen him in far alien ways

And known him by the terror in his eye,
The lofty forehead and the blanched cheek
And snowy beard disheveled, and the wail
Of his shrill voice upon the wind that cried
The while he fled from them.   And oftentimes
They told of his strange knowledge of the earth
And all that dwelt therein.   How he had seen
A wasp beside a rock a wall uprear
Of thin damp clay in tiny fragments borne,
And molded cunningly, until his home
The insect finished and was lord thereof.
And how he saw an ant in lusty soil
Bury a kernel that in time did bring
An hundred fold of kernels.   And from these
Learned how to build the city and to plant
The loamy wastes around.

                In lapse of time
The generations came that called him sire,
And spoke in pride that strong within their veins

There coursed the blood of Cain. And Lamech came,
The latest born of them, and sturdily
Grew to man's stature ; and his voice was Cain's
But had no tremor of a terror borne
Unceasing through the years, and in his eye
Shone the clear light the legends said of old
Was in the eye of Cain ere he afar
Fled from the wrath on High. And in his look,
Haughty and stern, the front of Cain was seen
Devoid of all its woe. And Lamech grew
The greatest of the young men of the hills
In knowledge of the fields and of the woods,
And of the signs of fruitage and the chase ;
Strongest in arm and fleetest of the foot,
And richest in the spoil the harvest days
Gave to the toil of tillage.

                    Love, since the ray
Of the first sunshine fell upon the earth,
Hath urged to passion all things animate.

And all of sentient nature thrills and sways ·
Beneath its touch of fire.   And Lamech loved
As loved the tigers that his arrows slew
Amid the reeds of Gihon.   Fierce and strong,
Yet restless and uncertain in his heart :
For of his tribe was Zillah, in whose face
And in whose form a royal beauty shone.
A virgin fearless in the woods and wilds
And skilled in learning of the fruitful fields :
Clear eyed and bronzéd with the far blown winds
And am'rous touch of sunshine.   Her he loved ;
Yet often thought how once in the dark night
He crept anear a watchfire on the plain
So still no watcher heard him, and he saw
Adah, the shepherdess, beside the flame,
Her fair face kindled in its transient light ;
And heard her voice low crooning on the air
A sad and simple song.   And saw her turn
T'ward where the star of even blazed and sank,
With wistful eyes and tender, ere her head,

She drooped in peaceful sleep.   All this he bore,
A picture constant in his wayward thought :
Yea, even while to Zillah his rude voice
Softened to tender accents, and he won
The pride of all the hills.   The marriage morn
Sank into crimson evening, and the night
And morning followed fast, and in his thoughts
As in his dreams the face of Adah shone.

Beside the flocks of Enoch, Adam staid
As was his wont.   And lifting his dulled eyes
Saw near a stalwart form, and ere he knew
Cried, wherefore comest Cain ? for he forgot
The centuries agone, and by him stood
One with the look of Cain and with his strength,
And with Cain's scornful beauty ere the Lord
Smote him in holy anger.

                    .   With a cry,
Such as the wild wolves make, the flocks were scared

So that they scattered. When, the turmoil o'er,
The sons of Enoch sought their place again
And called their sister, Adah, came no voice
To answer unto them. But far away
They saw the men of Lamech hasting fast
Toward the distant hills, and Adah's arms
Flung high to ask for pity ; and they saw
The strong-limbed Lamech turn and from his bow
Derisive throw an idle arrow back.

So Lamech outraged all the law, and sin
Lay heavy on his heart, and he grew stern
And bitter in his ways ; and to his eyes
There came Cain's haunted look. And day by day
He sought the mystery of the herbs that grew
Beneath his feet, and of the trees that rose
To give him shelter in the sultry noons ;
Of all the ways of beasts that trod the wilds,
And birds that winged in air, of creeping things,
Yea, and the changes that the flame could bring

Unto the very earth, as how the heat
Of the low hearth-fire turned the clay to stone :
And all were clear to him.   Yet grew his gloom,
For sin was in his heart.   And Zillah sought
To cheer him with her praises of his strength,
His riches in the fields, his valor shown
In dangers of the chase.   And Adah sang
Her shepherd songs to please him, and the tales
Of her own people told ; but bitterness
Was in the heart of Lamech.   All he knew
Gave him of pride and scorn, and oft his voice
Was raised against the shepherds.   So, they said,
Let us assail him, for a score can strike
Where one would fall before him.   Let us go
And smite him in the field.   They crept anear,
But Lamech heard the crackling of a branch
Beneath a careless hand, and drew his bow
And the straight arrow sent, and, lo ! a cry
Of mortal anguish to the skies went up,
While fast the foemen fled, save one who lay

With blanching face and red blood flowing fast
And breath that slowly ceased.

          And Lamech paled,
For never yet since Abel died a voice
Like this had risen to the Lord on high.

A little while he waited dazed and faint,
And saw the dry ground drink the crimson stream.
Then deeply digged the place and buried there
The foeman slain, and o'er him spread the waste
And old haulm of the vines. And Zillah cried,
They will return and slay thee ! and the words
Of Adah rose lamenting, they will come,
Thine enemies, and slay thee ! And they wept
Fearing the vengeance of the after days.

Then Lamech said : Oh ! women, hearken me,
I slew him who would slay me in my fields,
And mine own home I guarded. Even so

The eagles kill the hawks that seek their nests.

A vengeance seven-fold shall smite the head

Of him whose hand against our father, Cain,

Is raised in anger : and more great than this,

Yea, seventy-and-seven fold, the wrath

Shall smite the wretch that seeketh Lamech's harm.

And so consoled them, and the even came

With falling dew and coolness, and the dusk.

Then they their watchfire kindled ; and the dark

Gathered around its flame. The smoky light

Now rose, now fell, and swayed as swept the wind

With mournful soughing from the wilderness.

And as they sat beside it, high and far

A hound's shrill baying rose upon the air

And near and nearer came. They knew the cry,

For whoso heard it in the lonesome wilds

Or in the fens or in the stony wastes

Knew Cain was wand'ring there. For when he went,

A vagabond and outcast, pityingly

The dog that watched with Abel by the flocks

Followed his steps : for so the Lord had will'd
Lest Cain, forsaken and alone, should die
Ere he repentance knew.

The low fire sank
Its embers dulled beneath an ashen crust,
And still beside it Lamech sat and heard
The hound's deep voice draw nearer, while the dark
Grew deeper all around till from it came
The stately form of Cain, with hoary locks
And knotted staff in knotted fingers borne.
With furrowed brow, but in his sunken eyes
A light recognizant, as if a sign
Had drawn him hither for the welcoming
Of one with kindred thought.   And Lamech knelt,
For in those days men honored thus their sires,
And bade him welcome, and his vesture laid
Upon the breast of Cain, for now the chill
Of midnight lay upon the darkling air :

And Adah knelt, and Zillah, and their words
Were those that Lamech spoke.

　　　　　　　The hearthfire leapt
To meet dry branches thrown thereon, and soon,
The first words ended, in the flick'ring light
They sat in silence.　For the face of Cain
Bore look inscrutable, and fitfully
A dark gleam came into his eyes, and oft
Upon his lips wrath seemed to rise and die.
And oft he turned as if to speak, and then
Hushed the half uttered words.

　　　　　　　Until at last
Lamech, whose thoughts kept rhythm with his own,
Said, Tell the tale of all thy journeys past,
For I am Lamech, and my father, Cain,
Hath welcome in my home : and like to him
May be the sons of Lamech evermore.

Then Cain his hoary forehead bowed and wept
Ere he could answer him.

     Long centuries
Are gone since first my footsteps sought the wilds,
And seven generations from my loins
Have peopled these fair hills, and plenteously
They harvest of my wisdom in the fields,
And profit from the secrets I have drawn
From out the breasts of earth, yet not to them
The power to keep me from the wilderness
Or lure me to the ways of peaceful men :
To yield me shelter from the sun and storm,
Or share with them the thoughts that Cain hath borne
Throughout the weary years. So unto all
The lips of Cain are silent, and his thoughts
And memories he speaketh unto none
Save thee and thine.

      Then rose the voice of Cain
At first as if he knew a list'ner conned

The purport of his words, and then more free
As if in reverie.

I, the first born,
Beheld the earth mine heritage, nor dreamed
Of any sharing it. Upon my head
My father's hand lay kindly and his lips
Knew naught of chiding, and my mother's eyes,
Aye the soft eyes of Eve, gazed on me oft
In pride and benison, until he came,
Abel, my brother, whose low cooing words
Made my rough voice seem harsh ; whose winsome
   ways
To Adam's furrowed face brought eager smile,
And to Eve's eyes a look of deeper joy :
While I, neglected, sought the paths that led
Into the outland wastes, and brooded there,
Yet found dominion o'er the sheep that strayed,
And drove them here and yon. But as he grew
He called them from me with deceitful voice

So that they followed him.   And I who drave
Was powerless to lure.   So, in the wastes
He drew them from me and their spoil was his,
The fat flesh of the firstlings and the fleece.
And I, who in the wilderness had watched,
Had seen the flocks from out the herbage seek
The tasseled tops of that which highest grew
And eat the milky kernels, said, Behold,
When the hot sun upon the spires doth lie
And all its warmth is theirs ; when on the earth
Its fervor mingles with the dews below
There comes the greater yield.   And so I digged
And mellowed the deep earth, and all around
Drew forth the herbs of poison.   Soon I saw
The tremulous green leaves broaden and the spires
Grow higher in their strength ; and saw the ear
In deeper tinge of gold bend lower still
Beneath its wealth of kernels.   So I wrought,
And harvests that the earth had never known
Sprang from the toil of Cain.

Yet oft I gazed

Into the distance, and the idle sheep
The idle Abel followed in content,
While I in sun and tempest delved the earth.
And he knew naught save that the world was fair —
That suns were warm and pleasant, that the rain
Made sweeter herbage for his wand'ring flocks ;
That the high stars were kindly with their light
Sprinkled from blue skies when the day was gone ;
That long, sweet whistle drifted on the wind
Would make the sheep return, that murmured low,
His voice could call the wild bird from the wing
To nestle on his hand.

And I who toiled,

Who knew the secret that each wilding herb
Bore in its drooping leaves, and its root,
And in its bloom and fruitage ; I who knew
How bird and beast and insect built its home
And warred against the world, and lived its life

By dint of its own courage ; I who brought,
With mine own wisdom, from the sodden soil,
Of harvests fairer than had Eden known,
Was mocked of all his laughter idly cast
On idle winds afloat, from idle lips
Of him who loitered on the idle plains ;
While I was delving in the wearied earth
With weary heart and heavy, from the dawn
Unto the setting of the fervid sun.
Yet often when afar in dark were hid
His gathered flocks around him in the night,
I saw the twinkle of the fire he lit
Beside his resting place.   And well I knew
He looked toward the hills and saw the flame
Flicker and tremble on the distant slope
Where Cain, his brother, slept.   And in the day
I saw the wand'ring column of the smoke
Rise from the smold'ring brands he careful kept
Lest on the air the cherished fire should die
And all its light be gone.   And oft my thoughts

Of bitterness would vanish as I saw
The far flame glitter or the smoke arise :
For oft my heart was heavy in the fields
And lonely in the solitary ways.

The swift years came and went with scarce the sign
That wings of birds make in the river reeds,
Nor conscious lapse of time, until one eve
The storms arose and all the floods were high,
And the great rain came down and all the land
Was covered with the rain.   And all the flame
That he and I had kindled, and the brands
Low smoldering to keep the fires, went out
And died in darkness.

.

                  And the morning came
With calm, clear sunshine ; but no hearth fire blazed
Beside the hut of Cain or on the plains
Whereon the white flocks fed.

'Twas then we said

Forth from the darkling skies the fire doth come,

Launched from the Lord's right hand ; so let us build

Each one his altar of dry, crisping herbs,

And branches of the trees that storms have wrenched

From their deep hold in earth ; and on it lay

Meet offering to Him who fire withholds

Or gives it at His will.

And so we wrought

Each one to build his altar, and at last

There came a clouded eve when in the sky

The clouds were black with darkness, save when
cleaved

At its far edge the shiver'd shafts of flame :

And then our task was ended, and we laid,

Each on the altar builded by his hands,

Our offerings to the Lord. A firstling, grown

Without of care or labor, Abel gave

And invocation made with pleading words

That had the sound of cooing of the doves,
And wailing of the kestrels in the nest,
The soughing of the night winds on the plain,
And all things sweet and tender that may move
The heart to yielding and to kindliness.
And I of sheaves dragged from the stubborn earth,
Made fruitful by my labor, laid upon
My altar pile and waited ; and my voice
Was harsh upon the wind, for I who knew
To conquer by my strength had not of words
Wherewith to plead.

                    Then in the roar
Of the great tempest, when the firmament
Seemed rent in twain, and cloven the far sky
With broken bolts of flame, there fell the fire
And kindled Abel's altar.   And a calm
Came from the storm and the fair morning brake
And him the Lord had answered, but my sheaves
Lay drooping where the wind had strown them far,

And rain had beaten them ; and all forlorn
My altar rose dishonored in the light,
And I was wroth.

           I saw the lambent sun
Glow at the heaven's border in the east,
I saw it overhead and midway gone
Upon its daily journey ; but between
Within my memory no hour is lain
Or conscious is to me.

           But at my feet
He lay with his fair forehead bruised and gray :
And his dark eyes were closed, and in his hand
He bore the slender brand that he had touched
To the new kindled altar ; on his face
The kindly look he bore long years agone,
When in his childish play he brought to me
The gift of fledglings from a nest he found
Low sheltered in the herbs.

I gazed afar ;

And all the flocks were mine that fled from me.

The fair broad plains were mine inheritance,

For they were his no more. Yet not again

Should Cain look forth from shelter of the hills

And see the fair flame flicker in the night

To tell where Abel slept, or in the morn

The welcome smoke arise to mark the way

Cain's brother wandered in the pastures wide :

And sorrow crept upon me at the thought

That Abel's eyes should look on Cain no more.

And anguish came upon me and with fear

My heart grew heavy. And I bore him far,

Nor dared to lay the deathly burden by ;

Or knew how I should hide it from the sight

Of the all-seeing Lord. And agony

Grew strong and stronger as the days went on ;

And I dared not to leave him by the way,

For often as I went, I turned and came

And bore him thence again, till merciful

In their wild anger fell two ravens down
With beak and talon tearing, and one died,
And one did dig the loam and in it laid
The one he vanquished, and the brown earth
    smoothed
And went his way. So, seeing, thus I digged ;
Then over all my burden spread the earth
To hide it so away.

        Then on the wind
I heard the fearful whisper of the Lord.
And answered it deceitful. And I heard
The words of doom come forth from out the air.
A vagabond I went. My wand'ring feet
Found never rest among the sons of men :
Nor in the gorges of the wilderness,
Or on the burning plain, or in the vales
Where peaceful waters flow, was peace to me.
The flocks were scattered, but I sought them not ;

And the broad plains were fair but not to me
Was their sweet verdure pleasant.

Slow the breeze
Rustled the dead leaves of the yester year,
Crimson the embers sank, while here and there
A dry twig caught in momentary blaze,
Then fell and vanished.   And the light grew dull
That shone on Cain's dark face : and when his voice
Quavered and trembled at the last, he saw
That Lamech's eyes were hidden by his hand,
And Zillah's head upon her knee was bowed
In passionate sobbing : and soft Adah threw
Her arms upon his neck, and weeping cried,
Oh ! Cain, our father, would that we could bear,
Yea, we the young and strong, the bitter woe,
The guerdon of thy sin.

Then gloomily,
As if her pity stung him, with a smile

Sharpened with anguish on his lips, he laid
Her arms aside and rose.   His lofty form
Majestic stood against the darkened sky,
And the dull firelight gleamed upon his brow,
Upon his strong arms, and upon his hands
With knotted fingers clasped upon his staff,
And on his hair that wavered in the wind
That rustled the dead leaves.   Anon, his voice
Gaining new calm, he said :—

A vagabond
I went and wandered in the wilderness,
And by far rivers, and in mountain glens :
Upon the utmost summits of the hills,
Within dark caverns of the tow'ring cliffs,
In pleasant meadows, that with blossoms strown
Were like the vales of Eden in the tales
That Eve, my mother, told, yea, everywhere
I heard a murmur that was not of words,
Yet seemed to call to me—No more, no more

Peace cometh unto Cain.   And oft I said,
He cannot meet me in the darkling paths,
Or in the golden sun ; above him grows
The verdure of the plain.   Yet, oft his voice
Seemed mingled with the soughing of the wind :
And in the wakeful night I heard a step
That seemed the step of Abel, till its sound
Low died within the dark.   And then, again,
I said, he can not cry, nor can he tread
The fair earth any more.

There came a day
When, broken with sore travail, by the shore,
Far to the east, of ever surging floods,
I stood and marked the strength of rolling waves
Returning and receding, and the sand
Lay naked to the sun, and all the light
Of the high noon was there.

And on the sands,
Yea, on the bare shore, in the light of noon,

He stood, my brother, and his face was wan
With infinite sorrow, and no wrath was his.
Awhile he waited, then into the air
He vanished, and was gone.   The dusk night came,
And cool the far winds from the waters crept
Upon me in my sleep.   Again I saw
The troubled face of Abel, and his voice
Came to me in my dreams.   The earth shall writhe
As green leaves writhe in all consuming fire,
And in that day, he said, before the Lord
Shall Cain come forth for judgment.   And I woke,
And over me the face of Abel bowed,
Then faded in the dawn.

                    I rose and saw
On the high beach a tiny rounded clod
Tremble and break, and from its heart came forth
A creature winged and buoyant, and I knew
The Lord had sent a sign.   So, from the earth,
I said, hath Abel risen, and he lives

New-born within the air.   And Cain shall live,
Nor ever from his soul the burden fall
Of his undying sin.

                    Low Zillah cried
To hear the words of Cain, and Adah wept
Anear his feet, and Lamech's troubled eyes
Were cast upon the ground.

                    The voice of Cain
Again the silence broke, with prouder tone,
As if he scorned the sorrow that they bore
In sympathy with him.

                    Beside my feet
Lay myriad shells from the far deep upborne.
Of these I gathered of the small and great,
And with the gray sand filled them one by one,
Pouring from one to one until I found

That counting seven of the one it filled
The greater shell among them. And my sons
Measure the harvest kernels as the sand
I measured on that day. I saw a reed
Lie stranded by the waves. I broke it twice
And twice and twice again : and with it laid
A long length of the shore in certain space,
And with its parts I marked the lesser width
Of wet gray sand. Across my hand I laid
A fragment of the reed, and of the shells.
The seven little shells made balance fair
To that which greatest was, and so this day
Ye weigh the fatlings that your traders bring
From the white flocks of Seth : and whoso bounds,
The while the earth endures, his fruitful fields,
Or whoso tells the tale of harvests done
And gathered from the ear, or of the yield
Of fleece or flesh from patient flocks, shall share
The careful craft of Cain, for Cain hath drawn
This knowledge from the sea-shells and the reed.

Yea, more than this the thought of Cain that day,
Did grasp beside the sea.

A lowly nest
Close woven by the wild fowl, on the shore
Of the far heaving waters, loosed and went
Drifting upon the surge, and in it slept
The fledglings all unharmed the while the spray
Tossed white above them. And I said, behold !
Had Cain but ax more keen than flinty edge,
Slow sharpened on the rock, the lordly trees
Would fall beneath his strokes and he would shape
And bind their mighty stems, till on the wave
They floated like the nest ; and if there came
Days like to those ere Adam was. when all
The earth was waves and heavy darkness lay
Upon the waters, all the tribes of Cain,
Yea, and the sons of Seth, and all the fields
And woods have holden of the beasts that roam,
Would safety find upon them till again

The breath of the great Lord should lift the dark,
And cast the waves away.   Then, pondering,
I sought a river's banks and wove the reeds,
And clad them with the pitchy earth the sun
Softens beneath its touch, and lo, they rode
Upon the waters like the wild fowl's nest.

So, Cain, upborne, was master of the floods,
And in his wanderings no longer paused
Because of the wide waters.

From the shores,
Where the still river slept, the broad plain reached
Far inland to the hills, and high thereon
Grew slender shining reeds that in the sun
Glistened and shone, and when the tempests came
Bended and rose and writhing each on each
Made crackling in the wind.   There came a night
When Cain lay wakeful in the restless reeds,
And saw each clash on each until a flame

Sprang from their wrestling as the flinty stems
Ground one upon another.   Then he brake
A shining reed and strong, and as the wind
Clashed the high waving stems, he clashed again
The fragments in his hand until there sprung
A living fire forth from them.   And he bore
The flaming splinters thence unto the hills,
Clad with the arid grass, and touched the fire
To the dry herbage.

                    And the flame rose high
And the dark smoke was lifted on the winds,
Yea, even to the skies, and all the night
Was changed to light of day, and near and far
The mighty volume rolled ; the hoary trees
Were stricken so they fell, the pleasant meads
Lay withered where it passed, the lion's roar
Grew faint and further as he fled in fear ;
And all that could not flee, or bird or beast
Or winged or creeping thing, was seared and so

Was perished in the flame ; save Cain alone
Whose craft had brought the fire from out the reed
And launched it on the world.

And forth I went
And climbed the blasted hilltop in the morn
To gaze upon the plain, and desolate
Its blackened reaches lay, and at its edge
The flame crept cunning and the smoke rose slow.
And I, the outcast, Cain, exultantly
Looked forth upon it, for my hand had thrown
My anger on the earth, as from the skies
The mighty Lord had brandished forth the flame :
And Cain, the vagabond, had power like Him
Who kindled Abel's altar, and whose wrath
Doomed Cain a wanderer whose alien feet
Knew peaceful ways no more.

The wind more chill
Blew from the highland valleys, and the clouds

Grew darker overhead ; the embers' glow,
Half hidden by the ashes, grew more faint ;
Yet on the face of Cain their slender light
Was calm and steadfast, and his proud eye shone
Exultant as he spake.   He paused, and then
As if recalling all the sorrow past,
Spake with a voice more soft.   So Cain hath wrought,
Yet all in vain, because that Abel lured
The foolish flocks away, and unto him
Fell fire to light his altar long ago.

Then Adah spake.   From her wet eyes no more
Came the fast dropping tears, and slow her voice
Thus answered unto Cain :

                    Thy daughter's heart
Is full of anguish for thee, yet her lips
Must bear thee witness of the truth they tell
Who guard the flocks of Seth, where Adam dwells :
For he, thy father, knoweth all the tale

Of what befell ere Abel's altar fire
Rose lambent at the dawn to fall away
And perish ere the noon.

        The flocks were wild,
Scared by thy fierce cry : in the wilderness
They sought the mountain gorges, where the herb
Grew scant and thin upon the thorny slopes,
Where, when the wind swept from the wint'ry north,
They shivered in the storms. And Abel came
And drew them to the meadows of the plain,
Where water springs were gleaming, and the grass
Hid the white lambs beneath its lusty growth :
And when the winds were chill, within the vales
That opened westward, led them to the shield
And shelter of the rocks. And in the nights
When thou, Oh ! Cain, wast dreaming in thy rest,
He drove the wolves away : and so the sheep
Owned him their lord and followed where he went.
Yet never of their yield did Cain have need.

The flesh of firstlings and the woolly fleece
Were his for asking.   In the midnight dark
The fleece of Abel wrapped his brother's breast :
And the low roof-tree of Cain's dwelling bore
The fleeces of the flocks laid broad and slant
To shed the rain away.

Yet in thy pride
Thou watch'dst him scornful when his trouble came.
For well thou knowest when upon the marsh
He fed the sheep and murrain smote them sore,
Thou knewest herbs of healing, yet thy lips
Were silent unto him ; and when he mourned
Laughed low and mocking that he knew no craft
Of healing for his flocks.

And on the eve
Ye waited by your altars, Abel brought
The choice of all the firstlings ; but thine arms
Brought not the fullest sheaves to offer up

Unto the living Lord ; for all thine heart
Was covetous and vain.   And when there fell
From the high clouds of Heaven, flaming down,
The bolt that lit his altar, quick his hand
Reached forth a brand new lighted, that thine own
Might flash in joy beside him.   And he died
Unknowing of thy wrath.

The creeping wind
Swerved the light ashes on the smold'ring fire,
White as the locks of Cain : and gray the morn
Gave token of its coming.   In the sky
Clear shone the morning star, and sad the eyes
Of Cain were fixed on Adah, and he spake :
Oh ! Daughter, not in mine but Abel's ways
Thy spirit walks to-night, and thou hast kenned
Full many things that Cain has never known,
And Cain will hearken thee.

Behold ! She said
The morning star is passing, and its path

It keeps obedient to the hand that marked
Its place within the skies.   Shalt thou, Oh ! Cain,
Be more in thine own strength than is the star
That leads the hosts on high ?   'Twas long ago
Thy wisdom learned the marvel that the seeds
According to their kind bring forth their fruits
In harvests waited long : and so thy deeds
And all thy thoughts, Oh ! Cain, a heritage
Unto thy children be, and they shall bear
According to their kind.   Nor yet shall come
Full measure of them 'till the world shall end,
And harvests all be garnered of thy thoughts,
Of all thy purpose and of all thy toil,
And of thy passion and thy penitence,
Of all of good or evil that shall grow
From out thy wisdom of the woods and wilds
And from thy secrets of deep hidden things ;
Of all thy sons, unto the latest days,
May do because of thee, for in their veins
Shall flow the blood of Cain, and they shall toil

Because that Cain has sinned, and Cain shall bear
The burden of their evil : and their good,
Aye, in the last days of the earth, shall bear
A benison to Cain.

The level rays
Of the slow rising sun fell gray and cold
Upon their faces as the vibrant voice
Of Adah ceased.   The fiery eyes of Cain
Were dulled in weariness, and slow and sad
His gaze turned to the clouds that drifted on
Before the northern wind.   The hound uprose
As by a sign made conscious of the toil
Of wandering renewed.   And Cain his hand
As if for benediction, raised, and then—
Recalling that his lips no benison
Or prayer could lift unto the Lord on high—
Let fall the rugged fingers on his staff.
Then, to his glance obedient, Lamech came
And walked beside him, and they went away,

The hound close following.   Their hollow tread
Grew faint and fainter in the rustling leaves
'Till lost amid the murmurs of the morn.

Alone beside the ashes, worn and wan
With their long vigil, the two women staid :
And soft and low they spake, though none could hear,
In whispers shy and broken ; for each knew
The secret in her bosom, and the words
That Adah spake to Cain, to Zillah's heart
Bore meaning deep and strong, and Adah kenned
The truth of her own words.   So shall we bear—
They said in their soft converse—sorrowful
All that which Eve, our mother, bore when first
Woe came into the world.   In agony
Shall come the burden of our travail sore :
And care shall be with us while at our knee
Our children rise around us, yet their deeds,
Yea, when our hoary centuries are done,
Shall bear the fruits of mercy, and our thoughts

Sure guide the craft of Cain in blessedness
To all that dwell on earth. And in the day
The Lord doth judge of Cain, shall Lamech's sons,
And Lamech's daughters, rise, and all their gifts
Of good wrought unto men be brought and there
Made offering for Cain.

    The day was done
Ere Lamech came returning. From his lips
There fell no words of Cain, but in his eye
Shone dark the troubled look that Cain had borne,
And in his voice there seemed a sadness deep,
As in the voice of Cain.

    The fair fields changed
From the mid growth of summer, and the yield
Of harvest came, and slow to them again
There came the seeding time. And hour by hour,
Yea, from the mid-grown harvest to the spring,
The women spake of all the craft of Cain

And of his wisdom.   And they sought like him
To learn the secrets of the earth and woods,
And of the river beds and of the reeds.
Of the wild fowl whose rustling wings they heard
Startled within the forests.   And they brake
The hollow stems of herbs, and watched the toil
Of the nest-builders in the spreading branch,
And of the beetles that within the ground
Digged deep their tiny caves.   Oft Zillah strayed
To seek the marvels of the woodland ways,
While softer Adah crooned the dulcet songs
The brooding wild birds sang.

                    When bright the earth
Was all new born in beauty, and more strong
Because of the long lapse of restful days,
Did Zillah hide her in deep shelt'ring boughs
To know a mother's travail and her joy :
And Cain she called the infant, but in years

That came thereafter, when the molten ore
Swam at her feet in hollow molded loam,
She called him Tubal also. In the dell
Where the dun cattle pastured wild and free,
And thickets hid her in their dusky gloom,
Did Adah lie in sorrow, and she bare
Him whom they Jabal called in after times.
And never in the land of Nod were known
Two new-born sons of men with eyes more bold,
Or limbs more strong, or with more lusty cry
Than were these sons of Lamech. And he laughed
And said, so Cain shall live when Cain hath gone
Into the dark of death, and Lamech's years
Are vanished and forgotten. And the gloom
Went from his face ofttimes a little while
Seeing the joy of Zillah and the calm
That like the starlight shone in Adah's face ;
But sin was in his heart, and deeper grew
The look of Cain upon him, and he went
More often in the wilds.

Not yet the joy
That bent proud Zillah's heart to peacefulness
Was gone from her when once again she sought
The shelter of the boughs.   And Adah's lips
Bore smile upon them as she hid again
Within the thickets' shelter.   Zillah bare
Her whom they called Naamah, for·her ways
Grew into pleasantness.   And Adah gave
Another son to Lamech, Jubal called
When he had grown in strength.   Nor ever known
In all the land of Nod was gaze more soft
Than that of Naamah, a voice more sweet
Or dulcet cooing than from out the lips
Of joyous Jubal came.

And they were strong,
These children born of Lamech, and their strength
Grew greater with the fast returning days ;
And as the ripening harvests, one by one,

Came golden to the slopes the children far
And farther wandered from the hearth-fire's place,
Seeking the woodland ways, the river banks,
The mountain gorges and the dusky dells,
And reedy plains that hid dark silent streams
That crept from vales unknown.   And, day by day,
The lips of Zillah and of Adah told
How Cain dwelt in the wilds, and how he knew
All wisdom of the world beneath the skies ;
And how, one eve, he came where Lamech's hearth
Gleamed lowly in the dark, and how he stood
Majestic in the dawn the while the star
Of morning blazed beyond him.   And they asked—
These children born of Lamech—will he come
Again unto the hearth-fire, shall we see
Our father's father, Cain, and hear his voice ?
For so they knew that not in all the earth
Was greater one than he.   And Lamech laughed
With proud sad lips to hear them in their play
Speak thus the name of Cain.

                    Beside a stream
Where placid waters sluggish crept and where
The sedge grew high around them, Tubal Cain
One day led all the others, and they played
Beneath the shadows of high branching trees
That hid them from the sky.   And with the clay
Slow molded with their little hands they built
The semblance of the city, and the fields
That lay around its dwellings, and they made
Clay images, and one they Lamech called,
And one was Zillah, and one Adah was ;
The lesser were themselves ; and so, they said,
They peopled the fair city.   And anon
One greater than the rest they builded high
And in its hand a knotted twig they placed
As Cain had borne his staff.

                    Above them bowed
The lofty branches of the dusky trees,
While all was silent save their voices blent

With murmurs of the south wind in the leaves :
And slow from branch to branch a leopard crept,
The yielding branches swaying with no sound
Save of the rustling breezes.   Soft and low
The leopard slowly crouched and with its gaze
Measured the leap to earth.   A mocking cry,
In voice with scorn defiant, clove the air
As Cain from out the thickets came and threw
His look aloft and met the leopard's eye.
Then speedy fled the beast and far away
They heard its cry grow fainter till the sound
Was borne to them no more.

        Then fearlessly—
For they were born of Lamech—to his side
The children came and hailed him, and they saw
That he was Cain, for in his hand the staff
Was huge and knotted, and his hoary hair
Swept low upon his shoulders, and his beard
Was like the snow that lingered in the glens

When all the plains were green : and in his eye
They saw the gaze of Lamech, save more stern
Than his it seemed to them.

                    And loud they cried,
Saying, Cain hath come again and he will tell
To us the wonders of the woods and wilds,
And of the lands beyond the high blue hills,
Of those beyond the rivers and the seas,
And all below the skies.   Then reverently,
Their first glad impulse ended, low they knelt
Before the feet of Cain, for so they knew
Had Lamech knelt to Cain.   And thin and bright
Through the tall branches sifted, came the ray
Of the high noontide sun, and radiantly
Upon the brow of Cain it fell, and there
Lay soft and beaming, and upon his face
The rugged lines were softened as he gazed
On the fair children kneeling.   And he said,
Yea, Cain will tell ye marvels.   He hath come

To shield ye from the dangers of the wilds
Lest ye should die, and all the lore be lost
That he hath garnered for ye.   He will give
To ye the wisdom of his wanderings
That it may yield ye fruitage in the days
When him ye know no more.   For he is old :
He sees his children scattered on the hills,
And sees their tribes increase, and chief of all
Is Lamech, of his sons, and ye shall bear
The rule of Lamech when his days are done,
For all Cain's wisdom is thy heritage.
Then seeing that they hearkened in amaze,
Nor understood his thought, he spake again
In changed and simple words.   Ay, Cain is here,
So let thy hearts be glad, a little while
He lingers with thy play.

Naamah fond
Held close the hand of Cain, and Tubal threw
A mimic javelin to show his strength,

And Jabal gamboled with the hound that sprang
Elusive from his grasp, and Jubal sang
Of bird notes clear and soft, and rhythmic smote
A crystal stone beside him.   So they played
While Cain was watching, and the leopard's cry
Drew near and then receded and again
Came near and further went, until at last
Cain heard no sound within the forest depths
Save rustle of the branches ; from the stream
Naught but the murmur of the waters slow,
Moving along the sedge, upon its bank
Only the sweet child voices.   Silently
He stood and watched them, and his brow grew calm
And transient peace upon his forehead lay.
A little while he waited.

    Then he spake :
To each I bring my gift, yet bear to me
Each one his offering.   Let Jabal bring
From Lamech's dwelling the long twisted thong

Cut from the tiger's hide. A bow unstrung,
Yet with the strings of seven, Jubal's task
To lay within my hand, with seven reeds
The greater and the less. Naamah, bear
On thy weak shoulders the dark sodden sheaf
That lies among the sedge where waters flow
Sluggish and dark, and spread it in the ray
Of the noon sunshine here. Let Tubal's hand
Bring in its palm a fervent burning coal
From Lamech's hearth. Then fast the children sped
To do his bidding.

When their task was done
He looped the thong of Jabal, o'er his head
With strong arm whirled it, and with steady eye
Flung far the loop away and caught the hound
'Twixt limb and breast. Then loosened it and then
So flung it forth again, and taught the lad
Till he himself could wield it. So, he said,
May Jabal snare the wild bulls of the meads,

That stretch beyond the mountains, so may tame
The wildness of their strength.

Then Jubal came
With joyous step and lightsome ; from his hand
Cain took the bow unstrung.   The seven strings
He knotted side by side, and bent the bow
And strained the strings.   Then at his touch there came
From each a varying cadence, soft and low
As was the voice of Jubal, yet more light
Than cry of finches in the swaying boughs.
And Jubal's heart rejoiced.   The slender reeds
Cain clove across, the little and the great,
And laid them side by side and bound them so,
Then with firm lips breathed in them till there rose
Forth from the cloven reeds a sound so sweet,
So sorrowful and strange that all their hearts
Beat fast and wondering.   And Jubal grasped
The bow with seven strings and played thereon

As Cain had taught, and from the seven reeds
He brought the music forth.   Then Cain, to him,
Said, never while the earth shall know of joy,
Or know of sorrow, or of weariness,
Shall this thy gift be vain.

The sun aslant
Shone through the boughs, for now the noon was come,
And the dark nettle sheaves Naamah bore
From out the rotting sedge into the sun
Were dried and brittle, and their fibers gray
Hung loose upon the stems.   Then with his staff
Cain beat the gavels till the fragments fell
Splintered and broken, and the flax he drew
Into a slender skein and thence there came
A twisted thread more slender.   One by one
He drew the twisted threads, and then athwart
Of some he laid the others.   So he wove
And taught the weaving to the gladsome child.
Then Jubal, who with careful skill had laid

A crust of ashes on his open hand
That he might bring an ember from the fire
Glowing on Lamech's hearth, expectant gazed
Into the eyes of Cain : then at his word
He laid the crimson coal where steadily
Between two broken rocks the shrill wind blew
And fanned it into flame, then on it placed
The gray, dry driftwood that the floods had thrown
In spring upon the sands.

                    And while the blaze
Swayed in the wind and slowly sank and fell
Cain told this tale to him.   Ere yet thine eyes
Had gazed upon the world, one day I went
Where flame had scored the vales, and blackened lay
Its way along the edges of the hills,
And marked a rocky ledge where swift the wind
Swept clear and free, and lingering in the turf
Were little creeping flames ; but most of all

The embers of great cedars, in their midst

A dark brown earth, and slowly from it came

Dropping and creeping like to living things,

What seemed of molten stones, and in the track

Made by the wild hares' feet did flow and there

Grew harder than the stone.   I shaped a place,

Like to the flints on Lamech's arrows borne,

In shallow sunken sand and guided there

A tiny creeping stream.   It took the form

Of fairer arrow head than ever cleft

The air from Lamech's bow.   Between two stones

I beat it thinner and an edge more keen

Than broken crystal gained.   Then in the earth

I sought for hidden ores, and in the fire,

Amid the glowing embers by the winds

Blown into fierceness, placed them, and there came

Forth from their molten streams a fairer stone.

So came the iron ingots to my hands,

And so the brazen shapes, and these to thee

Are the brave gift of Cain.

Then when the flame
Was sunken into embers broad and deep,
And strong the wind blew from the low'ring east,
Did Cain upon them heap the dusky ore,
And on it lay the wood and then again
Heap high the ore, and then the wood laid high
Again upon it.   And the wind blew strong
And steady from the east, and from the pile
Like serpents creeping crimson to the sand
Flowed the thin streams of metal at their feet,
And purple glowed : for now the shade was come
With sinking of the sun.

Then Tubal said,
They tell not all Cain's wisdom in the hills,
Nor know it on the plains, for he who kens
The secret of this thing may rule the world ;
May smite the forest and may cleave the stone
And dig the earth ; and staves more potent make
Than those from oaken boughs, and make of blades

Shall cleave fire-hardened saplings as the stroke
Of flints the willow cleaves. Yea! he may rule,
Who owns this secret, as the tiger rules
The jungle and the fen.

Then Cain to him
Made answer thus : Shall Cain his gift repent,
Or shall he sorrow that to Tubal came
The greatest of his lore. Let Tubal's thought
Seek all the mysteries that hidden lie
Within the ingots, and their purpose seek
And all their uses in the hands of men :
Nor let them die with him, nor with his sons,
When he is old and passing to decay.
For I would have, when all our tribes are grown
To cover all the earth, that men shall say
That Cain lived not in vain, and so my name
Shall linger with my children till the days
When all the earth shall vanish, and the light
Of the high sun in sudden darkness die.

That noon had Tubal led the children forth,
Himself a child and buoyant in his heart
And careless in his thought.   The sunset rays
Were faint and fading where the waters plashed
Amid the willow stems, and now his face
Was gray in the dim twilight and no smile
Was bright upon his lips ; a youth no more,
He talked with Cain and understood his words.
Then slowly in the dark upon their way
The tiréd children went, but Tubal strode
With unfamiliar step and haughty eye
And voice of mastery.

                    Ere yet the slope,
Whereon the hearth of Lamech blazed and burned,
Their loitering footsteps gained, they paused and
        gazed
Back to the valley where the form of Cain
Grew darker 'mid the shade, and saw him pass
Into the forest darkness ; in his hand

His knotted staff firm holden, and his hair
Blown backward by the breeze that through the vale
Swept steadily and strong. And many a year
To Lamech's children came ere they again
Beheld the face of Cain.

And year by year
The fair tilled fields grew broader on the hills,
And year by year upon the pasture plains
The flocks more distant grazed. And year by year
To Lamech's foemen came a wrath more deep,
And fonder memory of him who fell
Beneath the hand of Lamech. Where the haulm
Of the dead vines was heapéd greener grew
The herbage in the spring; more heavily
Above the slain the yellow harvest ears
Nodded and drooped. And ever from the plains
The strong armed slingers came and rained afar
A storm of clashing stones. And from the hills
Came storm of arrows back, and so no more

Was death a stranger in the homes of men.

For men went forth to battle, and the cries

Of women followed them, and homeward came

And heard the cries of women.   Sad and slow

The living bore the dead, and in the vales,

And on the spreading plains, the haunts of men

Knew calm and peace no more.

               Then on the plains

The elder shepherds told how once the Lord

Had spoken unto men.   How Abel cried

That flame might kindle on the altar stones

'Mid tumult of the storm, and how his voice

Was heard in the high heavens, and they spake

With invocations loud.   And all the tribes

That dwelt upon the lowlands wailing cried

Upon the Mighty Lord, that he would shield

And shelter them from vengeance of the hills.

Upon the mountain slopes, in valleys far

From yellow teeming fields, in forests wide,

The dwellers in the hills the lurid flames
Of Tubal's labor saw, for he was come
To be a chieftain after Lamech's heart ;
And the deep craft of Cain within his thought
Had stronger grown, and from the heavy ore
With wind and flame he brought the metal forth.
He made of arrow heads and gleaming spears,
And broad, keen blades. And Lamech's heart was
      proud ;
For when the foemen came he smote them sore
With the sharp steel of Tubal.

             From the banks
Of the slow winding streams to where high hills
Sloped fair toward the sunset, grazed the herds
That Jabal kept.   For well his snares he threw
Among the young wild cattle, and their strength
Subdued unto his will.   And Lamech mocked
The puny flocks of Seth.   The women wove,

For so Naamah taught them, of the threads
From the wild nettle twisted, and the fleece
Brought, in the forays, from the plains below ;
And there was gladness in the songs they sang,
So that the heart of Lamech from its gloom
Ofttimes awoke, so he would laugh with them.
And to their voices Jubal's pipe was joined
In shrill and joyous music : oftentimes
The soft night trembled as the sound came forth
And dwelt upon the air, that from the strings
The hand of Jubal drew.   And dour and stern
Were all the sons of Lamech, and their sire
Was like to Cain in stature, and his eye
Gleamed like the eye of Cain ; and sorrowful
The look of Lamech grew when all alone
He wandered in the wilds.   And far the fields
Were smooth and green in summer, and their yield
Waved golden in the autumn, and between
The yellow reaches rose the city's walls
The hand of Cain had builded.

On the Lord
The shepherds cried as they to battle went,
And they who from the mountain came and fought
Raised high the name of Cain.   And to and fro
The tide of battle drifted, till there came
A day when back retreating to the hills
The sons of Lamech bore their captives on ;
And fleeing to far edges of the plain,
The shepherds bore of captives.   So the woe
And so the joy divided.

In that day
Was Adah agéd grown, and thin and fair
Her pure face shone amid the bronzéd tribes ;
And all her words were peaceful, and her thoughts
Were all of mercy, for her kinsmen they
Who dwelt upon the plain, and hers the sons
That strode in haughty vigor o'er the hills,
And bore the gleaming spears, and arrows drave
Like flight of birds upon the distant air.

So when they came, and in proud sorrow told
Of who was slain, and who was borne afar,
And spoke of vengeance on the captives brought,
Her words persuasive fell.

                    The earth of woe,
In these our evil days, doth have its fill,
And all is wrath and sorrow.   We who nursed
Our children with full breasts, and watched their play
With careful tenderness, behold them slain
Or borne away in bondage, and our eyes
Grow dim with weeping for them : yet ye strive,
And wrath is all thy portion.   Let them go,
These captives holden by thy vengeful hands,
That mothers wailing on the distant plain
May joyful greet to-morrow.

                    Ere her words
Were fully spoken, rose the wrathful sounds
Of loud remonstrance, and the spearmen knelt

To grasp of sheaves of branches bare and dry,
And heap them by the stakes where manacled
Their captives waiting stood. But clearer still,
Her voice rang in their hearing.

Hearken me,
The wrath of the great Lord is lingering
In the far deeps beyond the starry skies,
And whoso sheddeth blood, his blood shall stain
The verdure of the earth.

Then angrily
Did Tubal answer her. Behold, our fields
Were golden in the sun ; the thistles grew
And withered into stalks that, thin and parched,
Could catch the spark and bear the flames along
Until nor haulm nor many-bearded ear
Remained of all the yield. The shepherds lashed
High blazing brands on bounding foxes lured
From these our fruitful hills, and drave them back

So that the wild fire caught, and all our toil
Was wasted into ashes.   Shall we wait
And wail like infants while they loud rejoice,
These robbers from the plain?   And while he spake
A shepherd bound with withes, fair-haired and tall,
With steely light within his kindling eye,
Made answer back to him.

                    Ye seek our flocks,
Ye lure the fatlings from the shepherd's fold,
And seize the fleece, the fruit of all our toil
Through many a weary year : and like the wolves,
Ye creep in darkness, and we hearken ye
In the deep night, as hearken we the tread
Of leopards creeping from the wilderness.
And while upon the pastures lingers still
A lamb to tremble as thy footsteps fall
Shall all the shepherds hate ye, and their wiles,
Their anger and their labor on thy fields
Shall pour of evil forth.   Then as they rose

To smite him that he answered, spake again
His shrill defiant voice, Ay, smite, he said,
And gaze where yonder through the distant dark
A spark seems glimmering and faints and fails,
And then glows forth again.   There fagots lie :
Full soon around the stake their lurid light
Will flame aloft to heaven, and thy sons,
Yea, the brave sons of mothers in the hills,
Shall pay the bitter guerdon of the pain
Ye lay on me this day.   And Adah wept,
For so her children's children distant borne
Were captive on the plain.

             Then Lamech spake,
The while he leaned upon the brazen bow
That Tubal made for him.   What would'st thou have,
Oh ! woman, speak, and all thy will be done :
'Twas long ago I bore thee from the plains,
And Lamech's eyes are dim and Lamech's heart
Is full of gloom and sadness.   Thou wast kind

To Lamech in his brooding, and the storm
Of his stern heart hast lulled through many a year
Since Lamech's mocking arrows flew and fell,
Beside thy brethren's feet.   And so my will
Is but the will of Adah.   Let him die
Who scorns to do thy bidding.   And the front
Of Lamech grandly rose, and none save Cain
Had been so kingly of the sons of men ;
And all the tribesmen faltered, and the youth
Knelt low, and, fearing, listened.   Wondering
Hearkened the captives, till should speak again
The weeping Adah to them.   And beside
Strong Zillah stood and listened but no word
Her parted lips let fall.

     Then once again,
In softened tones and kindly, Adah spake :
Take from my pillow the fair whitened fleece
And raise it on tall pikes and bear it forth,
With hailing as for succor, to the plains,

So they shall smite ye not.   And with it lead
The captives to their home, so may their kin
And brethren yield to us our sons that now
Await the vengeful fires.   Then at her feet
The fair-haired shepherd knelt.

              The tiger's hide
That wrapped her feet he lifted to his lips
With rev'rent touch and fervent.   When he rose,
Strong Tubal, eager to atone his fault,
Upon a spear raised high the snowy fleece,
And round about the spearmen gathered close,
The captives following, and speedy strode
Down the steep slopes.   Then as the distant flame
Seeth'd higher t'ward the skies and scattered broad
Its newly kindled sparks, still faster sped
The messengers of peace.   And, nearer drawn,
They saw their brethren and the driven stakes,
And saw the fuel higher heaped, and then
They heard the clamor of the cries of war

And all the vengeful triumph of the foe.

Till, over all, the war-cry of the hills

Rose shrilly and defiant, and the heart

Of Tubal swelled to hear it, for it bore

No weakness in its tone.   And 'mid the sound

The captive shepherd whistled on the wind

A cry as of the hawk that frightened wings

Its sudden flight toward the drifting clouds ;

And whistled shrill again, and once again,

A signal wild and strange.

              Then suddenly

The baleful fire was quenched, and still and dark

Was all the night before them.   Then again

The shepherd whistled, but his tone more soft

Was varied on the wind, and answering came

A shrill, clear whistle back.   Fear not, he said,

They wait our coming ere a hand be raised

In vengeance or in wrath.   Anon, he sent

Another signal forth ; and one by one,

Dotting the outmost circle of the camp,
Low hearth-fires slowly rose, and clear and calm
The star of morning shone.

        The crisping herbs
Rustled beneath their footsteps as they strode.
The hares leaped lightly from beside their way,
And from the high mimosas came the thrill,
The song and cadence of the nesting birds
Awakening to the morn ; for slow the dark
Changed into dusk and dusk to silver gray,
And gray to golden beaming of the sun
Across the level plain.   And at their feet
The heavy dews lay crystal.   Where the fires
Had tawny shone within the dark, the smoke
Now lightly curled and faded.   And afar
Beyond the shepherd tents the lazy flocks
Were grazing in the dawn.

        So, peacefully
Before the sons of Lamech lay the scene,

And so once more the captive shepherds saw
Their dwellings near at hand.   And as they came
Rose shout and cry to greet them.   Marveling,
The gathered people saw the standard borne
Upon the spear of Tubal.   Half afraid,
As if some risen from the dead had come,
They saw their brethren, all unmanacled
And bright of visage walking close beside
The wild men of the hills.   Then mothers knew
That bale-fires of the mountains all their sons
Borne vanquished from the battle, spared, and so
Had let the lost return ; and high their cries
Mingled in fervid clamor.   From the limbs
Of their own captives all the bonds they brake.
Bright brands anew they kindled, and on high
They brandished them amid the mountain spears
And sang a song of gladness.

                    Yea, our sons
Are spared from battle, and, returned to us,

Shall lead our flocks anew. Their days shall be
As many as are Enoch's, he our sire
Whose voice has called upon the holy Lord
To save us in our trouble. Ay, we called
Upon the Lord our God, and He hath heard.

And while the shepherds raised the burning brands,
The women, clasping hands, with swaying steps
Danced joyous to and fro. The Lord doth keep
The tribes of Seth within His holy hand
To shield them from all harm. 'Twas so they sang
In rhythmic cadence while above them shone
The glitt'ring spears the men of Tubal bore.
And snowy high above them swayed the fleece,
Forever hence a sign of peace to them.
For now an agéd man came forth and slow
His weak limbs tottered, though the brawny arms
Of young men bore him up. His face was calm,
And his the eyes of Adah, save more stern
The look that lay within them. So, he came,

Enoch the chief among the tribes of Seth,
And all the clamor fell, and at his word
Was silence everywhere.

                Tell me, he said,
Ye brawny men and strong whose weapons shine
So glorious in the sun, how from yon hills
Shall leopards come in peaceful guise and lie
Unharming by our flocks : and shall ye bear
Thy spear heads wrought in fiercest flame and storm,
By crafty arts within the evil glens,
With peace unto us here.

                In Tubai's eyes
There flashed an angry light, but ere his lips
Could fashion answer, quick the shepherd spake,
He who had knelt at Adah's feet and heard
The blessing of her words.   Behold, he said,
We who are sons of sons of those who sprang
Forth from the loins of Enoch, in the field

Made battle 'gainst the warriors of the hills
And smote them sorely, and our brethren drew
Brave captives from the field, but overborne
Were we, thy children's children.   Far away
They bore us to the mountains : by their fires
Doomed they us unto death.   But over them
The mighty Lamech rules, and Lamech's heart
Is servant unto Adah, whom he won
By robber craft when thou, Oh ! Enoch, dwelt
A youth among thy flocks.

                    She ruleth them
With gentleness of heart ; within her eyes
Lieth the peace of those the living Lord
Hath touched with His deep pity.   To her comes—
'Twas so the hillmen whispered while she spake—
His voice forewarning in the brooding noons,
And in the fiery dawns, and when the eve
Falls dusk and cool unto the upland vales ;

And in the fearsome nights when all the skies
Are black with sudden storm ; and so she turns
The coming evil back.   And oft she hears—
'Twas so the hillmen murmured while we stood
Beside the kindled fires—His high commands
Resounding fall from Heaven when all ears
Save hers in wrath are closed.   And promises,
Wafted on gentle airs from where His Throne
Exalted stands, are borne to her in dreams
When all, save her, are sunk in sodden sleep
Forgetful and unknowing.   Her soft gaze
Is clear as waters that the melted snows
Leave in the peaceful hollows of the hills,
And her calm face is wan as is the sky
Transparent in the sunshine of the spring
Ere the low herbage 'neath the slender ray
Doth lift its spires anew.   And in her voice
Are tones of sorrow and of tenderness,
And mingled with them the slow strength of sounds
Like those the swelling rivers make when all

Their high shores yield unto them.   So she rules
The fierce tribes of the hills.

And at her word
They loosed our heavy bonds.   Upon a spear
Tubal, the son of Lamech, raised the fleece
And bore it hither, and he brings to thee
With it the words of Adah.

As he spoke,
Tubal stepped forth and on his forehead bare
The level sunshine lay.   The agéd men
Who long ago his father, Lamech, knew,
Cried out, beholding him, for unto them
It seemed that Lamech, to his youth returned,
Had come to speak with them.   Behold ! he said,
I, Tubal, son of Lamech, who is son
Of Cain the mighty father of the tribes
Who dwell in yonder hills, bear unto ye
Fair message of thy sister,—she who owns

The love of Lamech ; and her words are his ;
Let a white fleece upon a spear point borne,
As I have borne it hither, be the sign
Of truce and mercy in the strifes of men.
Wherever it doth come let arrows drop
Their points toward the earth.   Where'er it sways
Let the long shafts of spears their burnished heads
Uprear toward the skies ; and let the sword
In vengeful hands be stayed.

          Then, as he ceased,
The voice of Enoch answered, thin and shrill :
So let it be forever, and accursed
Be he that heedeth not.   And then the lips
Of all the old men answered, clear and high,
Aye let him be accursed.   And all the sons
And all the daughters of the shepherd tribes
There gathered in the sunrise, reverently,
And in half breathéd accents cried again,
Yea : let him be accursed.   And Tubal's heart

Swelled strange to hear the sound. His hand he
    raised,
As on the fury of a battle borne,
And, as in battle clamor, frenzied cried :
Aye let him be accursed. And at the sound
His kinsmen strake the spears, and to the skies
Rose their shrill voices, crying, evermore
So let him be accursed. And white as snow
In the fair morn the fleecy banner shone.
And on them silence fell as on the land
A calm descends when sudden storm is spent.

Then spake a captive, and the silence brake
With eager words and high : On yonder hills
Where Adah rules o'er Lamech's angry heart,
And where our brethren breathe with wrath subdued
But yet a little while, they mark no sign
Of all the mercy here. So, let us go,
And with us let the children of the plain
Bear back a white fleece high in air upborne

In token of our coming, so no harm
Shall meet us on our way ; and we shall bear
The message of the curse that Enoch spake
And Tubal and the shepherds.

                    Tremulously
The voice of Enoch rose :   From out the flocks
Bring forth a lamb unblemished.   On the pile
Of gathered faggots lay the sacrifice.
And while the smoke ascending, far and dark
Cleaves spiral to the skies, voice clear the song
Of rapture and of praise : and let the fleece,
From our burnt offering torn, be borne afar,
A symbol of the peace the living Lord
Doth will for all His children.   As he said,
So did the shepherds.   And beside the spears
The men of Tubal laid upon the sward
There lay the shepherds' crooks. And while the smoke
And odor of the sacrifice, on high
Ascended on the breezes, clear the voice

Of loud rejoicing rose in rhythmic tones
From sons of Enoch there. But Tubal knew
No meaning of their words, for in his heart
He praised the name of Cain, and like a dream
Dreamed in his childhood, and forgotten long,
Seemed all the sight of altar and the sound
Of sacrificial song. And mute he stood,
With all his men around him awed and still
The while the shepherds sang, and while the flame
Rose high and faltered, and to embers low
And then to ashes sank.

        Then forth they went,
The captives to their homes among the hills,
And with them shepherds eager for the sight
Of the fair city whence the sons of Cain
Ruled all the mountain vales. But Tubal staid,
And with him staid his men, and at their feet
Was laid the plenty of the shepherds' feasts,

And all the welcome of the shepherds' homes.

For they were kin to Adah—so they said,

The simple people of the plains—and so

Were kindred unto them.   And lingering

The warm winds touched the strength of Tubal's
     limbs,

And Tubal's spirit softened—and his voice

Grew gentler than of old.   And day by day

The men of Tubal languished in delight :

And spear heads rusted while the shepherd staves

Were worn with travail, and the rugged hills

Grew day by day more distant to their sight.

And better than the forges in the glens   .

To Tubal seemed the hearthstone, and more sweet

Than wailing of the winds that fed the fires

That smote the brittle ore, the dulcet tones

Of maidens' voices in the eventide

When sheep came to the folds, or in the morn

That waked the world anew.   So softer grew

The spirit of the wild men from the hills

In glamour of the fair and sensuous days
That softly came and went.

           And on the slopes
And in the valleys of the harvest lands
The shepherd messengers, at Adah's feet,
Heard words of peace anew.

           And so, again,
From one unto the other, to and fro,
The traders came and went.   And on the plains,
Soft voiced and lowly, peaceful shepherds spake
The name of the great Lord and cried to Him
In woe or thankfulness : but year by year
They cried the less to Him.   And year by year
Whoso amid the mountains dwelt recalled
The less the name of Cain.   And year by year
Their fair tilled fields were greater, and more great
The harvests than before.   And Tubal strake
Of spear-heads on the anvil, till more broad

And thin they were, and with them tilled the soil
With labor lightly done.   And Jabal's hand
Wearied the wild bulls that his leash had held
Until, obedient to his will, they drew
Of burdens o'er the earth.   Naamah wove
Broad fabrics that the shepherds sought, and so
Gave of their wealth of fleeces.   On the winds
Swam melody of Jubal's harp, and oft
His reeds gave solemn sound that far and sweet
Lulled into lofty rest.

                   So, in the glens
The flaming forges glowed ;   the captive herds
Bore burden for their masters : carefully
The women wove of fabrics fair and strong :
Alike in toil and restfulness the sound
Of music rose and fell ; and plenteously
The earth gave forth its blessings.   And the arms
Of the strong sons of Lamech held the maids

Borne from the shepherds' tents. The lowland
    swains
Wooed dark-eyed maidens in the highland dells :
And all were brethren in the peaceful days.

Yet everywhere—and year by year went on—
More languid were the breezes. On the earth
The sun more sultry shone. The winds arose
With more of sudden wrath, and failed and died
More speedily away. The rivers shrank
In fervor of the summer. When the fields
Were brown along the shores the torrents rose
And overflowed the land. From the low fens,
As year by year went by, the marsh grass crept
Into the upland pastures. High and far,
Where, in the youth of Lamech, all the year
The naked mountain summits met the sky,
Between the harvest and the springtide lay
The mantle of the snow ; and year by year
Lower upon the slopes, between the sheaf

And sowing of the grain, the tempest heaped
Its billowy drifts along ; and year by year
The drouth grew longer and the heat more strong
And latter rains more heavy.   And the heart
Of Adah weary grew, for boding fear
Was with her all the while ; and Zillah's voice,
And Lamech's, rose in wonder as they marked
The changes newly come into the world.
And spake of the old days when still there seemed
On hill and plain the winds that Eden knew,
And all the even verdure of its fields,
The soft calm of its skies, and balmy breath
Of wand'ring airs within the woods and wilds,
The storms that smote the night with kindled bolts,
And uproar of the skies that died at dawn
Leaving no wrath behind.

              And year by year
These changes came unto the earth and sky
And with them changed the fiery thoughts of men.

Their days were changed, and all their hearts were
    changed ;
And sluggish flowed their blood in slothfulness
Of dreamy drifting days. Of clustered grapes
They pressed the juices forth, and patiently
With careful, longing eyes, they waiting saw
The bubbles rise and sparkle, and they drank
And sank to dreams again, save here and there
Amid the shepherd tribes, a man arose
And cried unto the Lord : and in the wilds
Some rose and beat their breasts, and spake of Cain
The lordly father of a lordly race
Now sunken into sleep.

           And love and mirth
And sullen passions roused from slothfulness
To droop in sloth again, and wrath that knew
No noble impulse, and slow discontent,
And bitter scorn, and brooding sorrow filled
The languid lives of men,

And worn and old
In these last days was Lamech ; gray and wan
Was grown the face of Adah,—dulled the fire
That lay in Zillah's eyes, and Lamech's sons
Bore wrinkles on their foreheads.   And afar
The tribes of Cain were scattered in the hills,
And many cities builded, and their herds
Grazed all the midland vales, and far their fields
Were stretched on either hand.

At last there came,
Seething upon the air, the sound of strife,
Rousing the sluggish current of their lives
To those on hill and plain.   For restlessness
Of men grown weary of the pleasure born
From fruitfulness of harvests and the yield
Of willing herds and flocks, had willful turned
In anger on each other.   And again
The hillmen marshaled all their spearmen forth,
And those who drew the bow, and those who bore

The keen edged blades of Tubal. From the plains
Gathered the shepherd slingers as of old
In fiery marshaled ranks. And on the breast
Of mountain slope and level lying land—
For now were men grown cunning in their wrath—
There rose the ridgéd earth in ramparts high
With trenches deep behind. And from the plain
Came scoffing of the shepherds, and replied
The scorn of warriors from the citadels
That sons of Lamech builded.

Autumn came
And crowned an evil year with hoary frosts
More early fallen than the meads and wolds
Had ever known before. And when the rime
Was melted by the morning sun the herbs
Grew brown and sere, and all the forest leaves
To duller verdure changed. The sunset ray
Was gray and cold, and at the evenfall
The skies were cloudless and the winds were still,

And starlight came unheeded when the dusk
Had vanished with the day.

            In such a night
The shepherd sentries heard on silent airs
A cry afar, then wondered if they heard,
And listened that anew the sound might come
Assured unto their senses.   Then once more
They heard it faint and distant, and again
More near it seemed and shriller, till at last
A cry they heard like that the shepherd sent
Across the midnight air, the time there came
The men of Tubal with the fleece borne high
Upon their peaceful spears.   And in the gleam
And glimmer of the starlight soon they saw
The drift and sway of fleeces high upborne
With spear points bright above : then, nearer drawn,
Beheld strong sons of Tubal, fleet of foot
And strong of arm, but weary with the weight
Of hasting travail done,

And round them came
The captains and the wise men, and the seers—
For now 'mid battle slaughter, fervently
The shepherds called upon the Holy Lord
For safety and for succor.

Wherefore now
Come ye with symbols of old peaceful days,
Ye tigers from the hills ?   'Twas so they hailed
The sons of Tubal as anear they came,
But raised no hand to smite them, for the words
That Enoch spake, and Tubal, long ago
Were graven in their hearts.   Then sadly reared
His head the chiefest messenger, and spake,
And none from lips of warrior ever heard
Of tone more sorrowful :

Within our hills
In our chief city shielded, Adah dwells—
Then at her name the shepherds breathéd low—

And agéd hath she grown, and in her heart
Surpassing wisdom lies.   Around her head,
When the dim twilight comes, a halo shines
And wavers to and fro.   Unto her ear
Come all the sounds within the weary world
That meaning have to men, and to her thought
This many years the living Lord hath told
The mystery of His will : and yestermorn
She cried in her deep sleep, The voice is borne
Of Cain from vales afar, and with it comes
The baying of his hound.   And she awoke,
And listened 'mid the clamor of the birds
That sang in the high branches, and the shouts
Anon that rose when all our marshaled men
Looked forth upon thy people, and she said,
I hear the voice of Cain, and to her face
A look of anguish came.

And in the noon
When all was still, she listened and she cried

Oh ! Lamech, hearken ! for upon the wind,

Drawn nearer since the dawn, the voice of Cain

Is calling unto thee.   And softly, then

Our warriors paused and listened, but no sound

Came unto them upon the drifting breeze

That turned the leaves aside ; and they who seek

The leopard in his den and know his tread

That softly falls on woodland mosses, knelt

Low down upon the ground and hearkened there,

And, list'ning heard no sound.   And still she said

In anguished voice and weary, He hath come,

Though men believe that long ago he died,

And calleth unto thee.   O Lamech, haste ;

He calls for succor in the vales afar :

So, hail the lowland warriors, let them come,

And with our sons go forth into the wilds,

For Cain is calling sorely, and the hound

That walks beside his feet is baying loud

In watchfulness and care.   And while she spake

The air so silent was, that at our feet

We heard a locust creep, but to our ears
There came no voice from far.   Then Tubal said,
In angry guise, Shall we who rose the morn
To smite the people of the plains, go forth
Like women speaking peace.   Then once again,
As in old days, rose Lamech.   Though his eyes
Are sere and blinded by the years agone
A sound is sight to him, and to the head
The long straight arrow of a brazen bow
He drew to Tubal's breast, but Adah's arm,
Though weak and shriveled, turned the shaft aside.
With humble words knelt Tubal, and his voice
Was full of penitence, for so the sons
Of sons of Cain obey : and Lamech said,
Then let thy first-born bear the message forth
To those upon the plains.

            This Adah said,
Let of the wisest of their old men come,
The bravest of their young, and let them bear

Above their heads the fleece of peacefulness,
And let them with us seek the alien ways
Wherefrom the voice is calling : all the plains,
And those that dwell thereon, and all the flocks
Have profit of the craft the thought of Cain
Gave forth unto the world, so let them hear
The last words of his wisdom ere the earth
Shall know his voice no more.

And these her words
We lay upon thy hearts, and bid ye tread
With us in peace the paths where Adah waits
In sadness for thy coming.

When he ceased
A momentary silence fell on all,
Unbroken save by breathing hard and deep
Of those expectant waiting, till reply
Should from the chieftains come. These answering,
In one voice with the seers bid warriors raise

The snowy fleeces high.   And with them went
Foremost the seers white-bearded, and the sons
Of Enoch by their side, and following
Were stalwart slingers, and strong men who bore
The mighty staves of war.   And forth they trod
With sons of Tubal guiding, and the stars
Shone white and lambent o'er them.   Slowly rose
In the far north a wan and wav'ring light
From far beyond the plains.   And eastward kept
Toward the land of Nod their steady tread
Beneath the starry skies.   Yet as they neared
The foot slopes of the hills, a terror seemed
Far borne upon the air.   The night bird's cry
Was sorrowful and fearsome in the dark
Of the deep thickets ; and the wild wolf crept
Afraid athwart their path.   And when they came
To Lamech's dwelling, on the winding way,
The marshaled sons of Lamech bowed their heads
In sad recognizance.   Of forest boughs
And interlacing spears did Tubal's sons

A litter frame, and on it Adah bore
Foremost of all, save Lamech.   By his side—
For he was blinded, and his agéd eyes
Beheld the path no more—did Tubal go
And Jabal also, with their steadfast arms
Upholding as he trod.   But in his hand,
For so he willed it, Lamech's bow was borne,
The symbol of his power.   And Zillah walked
By Adah's side and held within her own
The thin white hands of Adah.   And behind
Strong mountain warriors followed, in their midst
The reeds of Jubal sorrowful and shrill
In measured cadence sounding.

                    And on, and on,
Beyond the stubble fields, beyond the glens
That glowed with Tubal's forges, past the meads
Where Jabal's herds lay sleeping, to the wilds
That hunters in their distant journeys knew
With steady tread they went, and as they passed

From out the forest depths the tiger crept,
The leopard and the lynx, and by their side
Came all the timorous beasts that in the woods
Had shelter from their anger, and there came
The fierce ones and the gentle in their fear,
And crept beside the tribesmen as they went :
For fear had banished wrath, and all alike
Within the brooding silence felt the woe
That lay upon the air.

                    So, onward trod,
The hoary Lamech leading and his sons
Gray bearded at his side, they who from Cain
And who from Seth had sprung.   And Adah, borne
Upon the litter, cried, I hear his voice,
The voice of Cain, low sighing, and the sound
As of a hound faint baying in the dells
Of mountains distant far.   And making haste,
The faster sped the night, the tribesmen gained
At last a level space whereon the light

Of stars unbroken fell, where all around
The shafts of high trees rose, with broad above
Their spreading branches thrown, and verdure deep
Was on the little plain.

And in the midst,
On couch of grasses sere and brown, there lay
The withered form of Cain ; upon his brow
Shone glamour of the starlight, and his eye
Was kingly as he gazed, but loose his hand
Lay idle by his staff.   Low at his feet
The gaunt hound wakeful watched.   Upon his breast,
Untouched by breath of wind, his tangled beard
Lay spread like drifted snow.

And as they gazed,
The tribesmen faltered and their cries went forth :
And Lamech, sightless led, knelt low anear
The weary form of Cain.   And by his side
They sank the litter down, and Adah's hand

Was on Cain's forehead laid and Adah's voice
Bore words of comforting.

                    At last he spoke,
The toil of Cain is ended, and his days
Are fading into dark.   A little while
He paused, and spake again.

                    Yea !   I have known
Through many centuries unto the earth
The changes come and go.   And evil came
And wrath and wrong and terror, and no more
Is peace within the world.   Yet it shall come
Through many marvels and through evil days
And anger of the Lord.   Ay !   Year by year
The waters of the mighty seas are borne
By ardor of the sun and sweeping winds,
And gather, in the snows, and in the earth
Are hidden deep away.   So, year by year,
The lowland herbs upon the heights are grown

And river birds are nesting in the hills.

Where long ago I Lamech's children sought,

Upon the banks where pleasant waters flow,

Beside my way I found a hoary stone

Engraven with the stars, for so of old

The sons of Seth were wise and marked the place

Of all the stars on high.   Then curiously

I gazed upon the skies and, lo ! no more

The stars were where they were.   And all is changed

And changing on the earth, and in the skies

The hosts of heaven change.

"Twas so I said

And, pondering, I slept ; and in my sleep

A dream came to me and I saw the earth

And all that is therein : and high the waves

Did rise upon the mountains, and the hills

Were hidden by the waves, and slowly rose

Unceasing in their strength the mighty seas ;

And all the mountains vanished, and I cried

Lo ! They are gone, my children, and again,
I cried, lo ! they are gone who sprang from Seth,
Seth, he, my brother, who for Abel slain
Was come into the world.   And in my woe
I cried unto the Lord, and, lo ! my dream
Was changed, and on the waters drifting far
Mine eyes beheld the reeds that long ago
I launched upon the billows, and, behold !
Upon them were the children Adah bare,
And those of Zillah, and the sons of Seth,
His shepherd daughters, and his lingering flocks,
Yea, and the beasts that in the wilderness
Had known the face of Cain, and with them lay
Upon the reeds the herds that Jabal drave
With burdens borne upon them, and my heart
Went forth in thankfulness.

          And I awoke.
Then all the air was still and all around
No leaf stirred in the branches.   Calm the stars

Looked down upon me, and there seemed to fall
From out the firmament a tender voice
That whispered slowly.   Yea, the time hath come
And Cain is penitent, so may he know
The marvels yet to be.

> Then on my eyes
Soft sleep did come again, and in my dream
The waves receded and the land came forth ;
And on our plains, yea, far beyond the seas
That lapse upon the borders of our land,
I saw fair harvests gleam, and cities rise :
And on the narrowed waters proudly rode
Fair wide winged birds that, floating, proudly bore
From shore to shore the harvests and the yield
Of forges like to Tubal's, save their smoke
Was as the storm clouds that the strong wind drives
Ere fire doth cleave the skies.

> Then nearer drew
The distant lands unto me and I heard

Soft voices of their peoples, sweet and clear
As was the voice of Abel ; and I saw
Their faces in the light, and on them lay
The peace that Abel knew.   And in my heart,
Lo ! he doth live, I said, his gentleness
Is heritage of these.

       So, in my dream
I, Cain the wanderer, the marvel saw
And I was comforted.

       Again I woke.
Mine heart was fain that Lamech came to me,
That Lamech's people came, and Enoch's sons,
So they might hearken me : and so my voice
Rose crying on the air, for I am old
And now my day is ending, and the dark
Is coming fast to me.

       On Adah's knee
Cain's hoary head was lain ; his eyelids sank

And thinner grew his face.   And silent all
The tribesmen knelt around him.   On his brow
Fell the dim starlight.   To the zenith far
The streaming light arose that at the eve
Had waver'd in the sky.   Upon his face
There came a stony calm.   And Adah wept,
And all the warriors wept, and from the wild
Loud wailing rose, for all its denizens
Had known the heart of Cain.

              But grief most strong
Must cease, as mighty storms must fail and faint
And fainter grow till calmness comes and gleams
In transitory peace while yet the boughs
Wind broken quiver in the eddying winds,
And so the wailing ceased.   The tribesmen digged
With spears inverted till a grave they made
Full deep and broad, and in it laid the turf
Clean cloven from the ground, and carefully
Upon it spread the fleeces from the spears

The lowland shepherds bore. The form of Cain
They placed within the grave with gentle hands,
And spread the fleeces that were borne on high
By Tubal's stalwart sons, upon his breast
To shield him from the loam. And noting then
The faithful hound was silent and no breath
Came from his nostrils, they within the grave,
Beside the feet unshod, low laid him down,
As in the wilderness his watch he kept,
To guard the sleep of Cain.

                    And over all
They heaped the mellowed earth. From all around
Of boulder stones they brought, and built a cairn
With sides steep sloping, one toward the place
Where clear the north star shone, and southward one
Toward the billowy seas ; and one there was
Fair faced toward the west where late arose
The lambent star of even, and one lay
Aslant toward the dawn. And like to this,

Spake Tubal as they toiled, shall be the tombs
Of conquerors and kings until the world
Shall know of man no more.

And gray and cold
The daylight broke upon them as they turned
Unto the land of Lamech and the plains
That lay beyond his fields. And noon was high
In clear calm skies when from the hills they saw
The shepherd tents below.

Then every one
Of all the lowland tribesmen went his way,
And slowly night drew near ; and silently
Unto his hearthfire Lamech's children came.
And Lamech by it brooded, by his side
The strong limbed Zillah stood, and on her couch
Lay Adah wearied, and afar the wind
Made murmur with sere leaves, and with the grass
That higher grew where long ago was spread

The dead haulm of the vines.   The firelight shone
Fitful upon their faces.   Silently—
Save for the low sound of the wind—the night
Grew deeper and more dark.   Then Adah brake
The sorrowing silence, and her voice was clear
As tones of one rejoicing.   Nevermore
Upon the earth shall dawn of morning come
Unto the eyes of Adah.

Come to me,
Oh ! Zillah, kneel as long ago we knelt
Ere these our bearded sons their infant lips
Had touched upon our breasts.   And dream not thou
That our fond thought was vain.   Through centuries
The guilt of Cain shall soften, for the toil
Of Lamech's children in its yield shall bear
For him atoning harvests.

Though the floods
As Cain beheld them in his dream shall rise

Above the mountain summits, softly borne
Shall men outride the tempest, for his thought
Hath safety shaped for them. And everywhere
The craft he taught our children, in the fields
And in the forest wilds, and by the shores
Of far resounding seas, and on fair plains
That know no shadows of high branching boughs,
And in waste places of the earth, and far
Toward the northern stars in lonely isles,
And lands afar where slow the sunset burns
Beyond our farthest ken, within the hearts
Of men shall bear its fruitage, and their hands
Shall gather golden harvests all their days
And earth be glad to them.

And lest the woe,
The travail and the tempest yet to be,
Bring death unto our race, and so be lost
The mighty wisdom of the tribes of Cain,
Let their fair daughters wed the lowland swains

Who guard the flocks of Seth, and let their sons
Wed with the maidens, who with ardent eyes,
Behold the stars and in the far skies trace
Their paths above the plains ; and so the seed
Of Cain shall linger to the latest day
That shines upon the world.

                        And all the thought
Of all the sons of Cain shall give its yield
According to its kind, and all the toil
Of Lamech's sons, that greater harvests bring,
Lighten the woe of men.   And all the peace .
That, joyous born of plenty, to the earth
Shall come because of them, shall multiply
According to its kind.   And men shall learn
Because of them, to trace the wayward winds,
And mark the slender beetles of the clay ;
To note the creeping herbs, and in the stones
Find many marvels, till their voices rise

In praise unto the Lord that He hath wrought
The wondrous world for them.

And at the last,
When all the glory of the Lord shall shine
In calm clear light above the lurid flame
That all the earth consumes, and at His feet
They who have waited long for judgment come,
The sons of Lamech and their sons shall bear
To Him their offering of all their toil
Hath done of good to men, a sacrifice
For all the guilt of Cain.

And from the Throne,
The Throne of the great Lord, shall come a voice
He hath atonement made through Zillah's sons
And through the sons of Adah.   Then shall rise
The voice of Abel with the throngs that sang
With morning stars together ; and the guilt

Borne through the weary years shall fail and die,
And Cain, redeemed, shall stand before the Lord.

Pale grew her lips and thin her veinéd hands,
Gray was the shadow on her face that crept
And on her closéd eyes.   And on her brow
Serene and soft the star of even shone.

FINIS.

www.ingramcontent.com/pod-product-compliance
Lightning Source LLC
Chambersburg PA
CBHW022339020726
47500CB00004B/1192